THE Best FATHER'S DAY PRESENT Ever

CHRISTINE LOOMIS

pictures by

PAM PAPARONE

 G. P. PUTNAM'S SONS

G. P. PUTNAM'S SONS A division of Penguin Young Readers Group. Published by The Penguin Group. Penguin Group (USA) Inc., 375 Hudson Street, New York, NY 10014, U.S.A. Penguin Group (Canada), 90 Eglinton Avenue East, Suite 700, Toronto, Ontario, Canada M4P 2Y3 (a division of Pearson Penguin Canada Inc.). Penguin Books Ltd, 80 Strand, London WC2R 0RL, England. Penguin Ireland, 25 St. Stephen's Green, Dublin 2, Ireland (a division of Penguin Books Ltd.). Penguin Group (Australia), 250 Camberwell Road, Camberwell, Victoria 3124, Australia (a division of Pearson Australia Group Pty Ltd). Penguin Books India Pvt Ltd, 11 Community Centre, Panchsheel Park, New Delhi - 110 017, India. Penguin Group (NZ), Cnr Airborne and Rosedale Roads, Albany, Auckland 1310, New Zealand (a division of Pearson New Zealand Ltd). Penguin Books (South Africa) (Pty) Ltd, 24 Sturdee Avenue, Rosebank, Johannesburg 2196, South Africa.

Penguin Books Ltd, Registered Offices: 80 Strand, London WC2R 0RL, England.

Published simultaneously in Canada. Manufactured in China by South China Printing Co. Ltd. The art was done in pen and ink with watercolor.

Design by Gina DiMassi and Marikka Tamura. Text set in Rekord Black.

Library of Congress Cataloging-in-Publication Data

Loomis, Christine. The best Father's Day present ever / Christine Loomis ; illustrated by Pam Paparone. p. cm. Summary: Langley the snail arrives at the store too late to buy the perfect Father's Day present for his dad, but on the return trip, he finds that the very best gifts are from the heart. [1. Gifts—Fiction. 2. Father's Day—Fiction. 3. Snails—Fiction.] I. Paparone, Pamela, ill. II. Title. PZ7.L874Be 2007 [E]—dc22 2006003605 ISBN 978-0-399-24253-3

1 3 5 7 9 10 8 6 4 2

First Impression

For my dad, Donald Hutchins Loomis;
thanks for the memories.
—C. L.

For (who else?) my father.
—P. P.

It was almost Father's Day. Langley had not found the perfect present for his dad. Again.

"Your father doesn't care about expensive gifts," Langley's mother said for the 500th time. "Make him something. He'll like that."

But everything Langley ever made was a disaster. One year he painted a picture of his dad's favorite spot by the stream. It looked like a bluish-purplish monster dripping blue ooze from its lumpy head.

Then there was the picture
frame stuck with gluey macaroni.
"Very . . . creative," his teacher
had said.

Last year, Langley made a paperweight for his dad
to take to work. It looked good. Unfortunately, his dad
didn't have a desk at work.

"I love it," Mr. Snail had said. But Langley didn't believe him.
He spent the rest of that day in his room, staring in the mirror
to see if he looked as dumb as he felt.

This year was different. Langley had an allowance. He was thinking of what he might buy—A bowling ball? Bow tie? A hiking boot?—when Buster Squirrel ran up. "We're going to Mister Pockets' store. Wanna come?"

Eureka! Langley's worries were over. Mister Pockets carried the coolest gifts, gadgets and doodads. Langley would find the best Father's Day present ever.

Langley counted his money. When he looked up, Buster was far down the road. Everyone else passed him, too.

"Sorry, can't wait," Chloe Rabbit called as she leapt by. "Gotta get to Mister Pockets' store." Todd Toad hop-flopped past with a wave.

Soon Langley's friends reappeared—coming the other way!

"Look what I got," Buster said, pulling a strange contraption out of a bag.

"What is it?" Langley asked.

"A Turbo-Blaster-Car-Washer-and-Ice-Cream-Maker."

Langley wondered if his dad would like that.

"I got the last one," Buster said.

Chloe had
a Super-Duper-
Golf-O-Matic-
Home-Ball-Washer,

and Todd's gift was professionally
wrapped in eye-catching
colored paper.

"It's the Amazing Auto-Select-
Sports-Only Remote Control with
batteries included," Todd said
proudly.

Langley raced up to Mister Pockets' store. A large sign stopped him cold in his track.

CLOSED EARLY

FOR FATHER'S DAY

WEEKEND

mister Pockets ®

Langley was stunned. Tomorrow all the dads would be out polishing their cars and making ice cream or washing golf balls until they sparkled or amazing their friends with the Sports-Stations-Only Remote Control with batteries included. Except Langley's dad.

"I'm such a **LOSER**," Langley wailed.

Sadly, he turned away from the store and headed back the way he had come. Then he spotted something in the road. It was a lilac-colored rock with a perfect white circle around it. "Dad says circle rocks are good luck," Langley sniffed, placing the rock in his pack.

Oddly, he felt better. He started home at a snail's pace.

Which is why he noticed the cupped leaf holding
a perfect puddle of water that reflected a circle of
bright blue sky. Dad would like this, Langley thought.

A short while later, a speckled eggshell caught his eye.
A riot of chirping made him look up at a neat twig nest.
"Welcome to the world," Langley called to three little
birds, because that's what his dad would have done.

When he stopped to rest, a large
web at the end of the log sparkled
in the coppery sun.

Suddenly, Langley knew just
what to give his dad.

The next morning, he placed his gift on the table. It wasn't a Turbo-Blaster-Car-Washer-and-Ice-Cream-Maker or Super-Duper-Golf-O-Matic-Home-Ball-Washer or Amazing Auto-Select-Sports-Only Remote Control with batteries included. It wasn't professionally wrapped in eye-catching colored paper.

"What's this?" Mr. Snail said as he opened the small, oddly shaped parcel covered in old paper with X's marked on it. Inside was the lilac-colored rock and a note saying:

Langley took
his dad to see the
sparkling web.

Together
they called up
to the three
little birds.

They drank from the dark green leaf
with the puddle of bright blue sky, and
Langley pointed out exactly where he
found the good-luck rock. They took lots
of pictures. It was a perfect day.

As they turned into their shady yard,

Langley asked, "Dad, did you like your present?"

Mr. Snail gave his son a great big snail hug.

"It was the best Father's Day present ever!"

And Langley knew that it was.